when DINOSAURS came with everything

when
DINOS

AURS

came with everything

written by Elise Broach

illustrated by David Small

SIMON AND SCHUSTER

LONDON   NEW YORK   SYDNEY

SIMON AND SCHUSTER

First published in Great Britain in 2008 by Simon & Schuster UK Ltd

Africa House, 64-78 Kingsway, London WC2B 6AH

A CBS company

Originally published in 2007 by Atheneum Books for Young Readers,
an imprint of Simon & Schuster Children's Publishing Division,
New York

Book design by Dan Potash
The text for this book is set in P22 Stanyan Bold.
The illustrations for this book are rendered in watercolour and ink.

A CIP catalogue record for this book is available from the British Library

ISBN -13: 978-1-84738-193-4

Printed in China
10 9 8 7 6 5 4 3 2 1

For Ward, in honour of
all our family trips
to the American Museum
of Natural History
–E. B.

To Lily
–D. S.

Friday is a very busy day.
Mum goes on lots of boring errands, and I have to go with her.

And this Friday seemed like every other
Friday . . . until we got to the bakery. A sign
above the doughnuts read:

I couldn't believe my eyes. Neither could Mum.
"They *must* mean a toy," she said.

But when I took the box of doughnuts, the lady
behind the counter said, "Hold on, little fella.
Don't forget your dinosaur."

And
there
he was!

"Mum!" I yelled. It was a triceratops.

"What!" cried Mum. She did not look happy.
"How are we supposed to get *that* home?"
The bakery lady smiled. "Oh, don't worry, he'll follow you.
They always do."

And he did . . . all the way to the doctor's, where I had to go for my checkup.

Mum shook her head. "What are we going to do with him now?" She looked him up and down.

That took a while.

"We can't take him inside," she said finally. "He'll have to stay in the car park."

I told him not to talk to strangers.

After my checkup, I asked for a sticker, like usual.
"No stickers today," said the nurse. "Just dinosaurs.
With every injection, you get two."

"I want an injection," I said.

The nurse smiled. "Not today, young man. But you
can pick up your dinosaur at the front desk."

"Mum!" I yelled. There, at the front desk,
was a stegosaurus.
    "What on earth is going on?" Mum cried.
    "It's a special day," the nurse explained.
"Today, dinosaurs come with everything!"

    "Yessss!" I said.
    "Noooo," Mum groaned.

We walked down the street, and my triceratops and my
stegosaurus walked right behind us.

THUD,   THUD,   THUD.

They made friends straight away.

Across the street, other kids had
dinosaurs too. I saw an ankylosaur,
a duckbill, and a velociraptor. We
all waved at each other. Our mothers
glared and kept on walking.

"I think we'd better go home right now," Mum said.
"But what about my haircut? The hairdresser's waiting for me."

Mum looked at the dinosaurs. Then she looked at my hair. "The
hairdresser always gives you a balloon, doesn't he? A nice balloon?"
"Uh-huh," I said.
I didn't want a balloon.
I wanted a barosaur.

At the hairdresser's, I gave my triceratops and my
stegosaurus doughnuts for a snack. They waited outside
and watched through the glass.

The hairdresser pumped the chair up high. He cut my hair too short, but I
didn't mind because then he patted my head and said, "Wait right here, son."

He was gone for a long time. Mum tapped her foot. "I don't like this," she
said. "Where exactly do they keep the balloons?"

Just then, the hairdresser came back with something flying over his head.
It wasn't a balloon.

"Mum!" I yelled. It was a pterosaur.

"This is too much," Mum protested.

"Now, listen," she said to the hairdresser. "I think a balloon
will be enough today. Don't you have any balloons?"
"Sorry, madam. No balloons. You get one of these instead."

It was like that everywhere we went.
At the shoe shop, the sign read: BUY TWO PAIRS, GET DINOSAUR FREE!
Mum decided my shoes would last a while longer.

At the cinema, we could hear the popcorn man shouting,
"Toffee? No Toffee? You want a dinosaur with that?"
Mum said we'd go another day.

At the diner, I wanted to stop for a hamburger.

But then a girl walked out
with a *tyrannosaurus rex*.

"Okay, that's it!" Mum cried. "We are definitely not having lunch there."

She looked at my triceratops, my stegosaurus, and my pterosaur. "What are we supposed to do with all of these dinosaurs? We don't have room for them! We can't take care of them!"

I hugged her leg. "Don't worry, Mum. They can live in the back garden!"

Mum shook her head. "Sweetheart, they're not toys. Dinosaurs are a lot of work."

"But, Mum, look! They eat anything. And they sleep outside. I'll do everything, I promise. Please, Mum? Please?"

Mum sighed.

"Well, I suppose we can't just leave them here. Thank goodness we didn't stop at the diner."

We hurried home, and my dinosaurs hurried after us.

THUD, THUD, THUD. FLAP, FLAP, FLAP.

When we were almost there, we saw a little duckbill dinosaur, standing alone on the street corner. He looked lost.

"Mum, that's a baby hadrosaur. He's all by himself!"

"Sweetie, we've already got our hands full."

The hadrosaur followed us.
It wasn't my fault.

When we got home, Mum needed to lie down, so I
made lunch for the dinosaurs.

Then I showed them where their toilet was.

I told them to stay out of the neighbour's garden because of his mean dog.

And I showed them my slide, my tyre swing,
and all the toys in the garage.

They seemed to be having fun, but they really went
wild when I took out my Frisbee.

The hadrosaur had the first throw. The Frisbee landed
on the roof. I saw Mum watching from the window.

"Is everything all right out there?" she asked.

"Everything's fine, Mum. We can get it down." And my
pterosaur flew up and plucked the Frisbee out of the gutter.

Mum kept watching.
She looked at him for a long time.

The next thing I knew, she
had him cleaning the gutters!

Then she came out to the back garden with a pile of wet clothes.
"These spikes come in handy, don't they," she said.

Pretty soon, Mum had thought of chores for all of my dinosaurs.

But I knew they didn't mind. It just meant they were part of the family.

When we were finished helping, Mum said I could invite some friends over. It was a bring-your-own-dinosaur party!

And guess what
happened next?

I heard Mum on the phone to the bakery.
She asked, "Do you have any doughnuts left?"

And that's when I knew
everything would be okay.